SNOW TRUCKING!

WRITTEN BY JON SCIESZKA

CHARACTERS AND ENVIRONMENTS DEVELOPED BY THE

DAVID SHANNON   **LOREN LONG**   **DAVID GORDON**

ILLUSTRATION CREW:

Executive producer: TOT INDUSTRIES in association with Animagic S.L.

Creative supervisor: Sergio Pablos ○ Drawings by: Juan Pablo Navas ○ Color by: Isabel Nadal

Color assistant: Gabriela Lazbal ○ Art director: Karin Paprocki

READY-TO-ROLL

ALADDIN PAPERBACKS

NEW YORK   LONDON   TORONTO   SYDNEY

🐦 ALADDIN PAPERBACKS

An imprint of Simon & Schuster Children's Publishing Division
1230 Avenue of the Americas, New York, NY 10020
Copyright © 2008 by JRS Worldwide, LLC
The text of this book was set in Truck King.   Manufactured in the United States of America
 10 9 8 7 6 5 4
Library of Congress Cataloging-in-Publication Data
Scieszka, Jon.   Snow trucking! / by Jon Scieszka ; artwork created by the Design Garage:
David Gordon, Loren Long, David Shannon.—1st Aladdin Paperbacks ed.
p. cm.—(Jon Scieszka's Trucktown. Ready-to-roll.)
Summary: On a snow day, all the trucks go out to play.
ISBN-13: 978-1-4169-4140-8   ISBN-10: 1-4169-4140-1 (pbk)
ISBN-13: 978-1-4169-4151-4   ISBN-10: 1-4169-4151-7 (library)
 [1. Trucks—Fiction. 2. Snow—Fiction] I. Design Garage. II. Gordon, David, 1965 Jan. 22- ill.
III. Long, Loren, ill. IV. Shannon, David, ill. V. Title.
PZ7.S41267Sn 2008   [E]—dc22   2007027152

Monday.
Snow.

Tuesday.
SnOw.

Wednesday.
"Snow day?" asks Jack.

Ted's radio beeps.
Beep beep beep.

"Snow day!"
the radio beeps.
"Snow day!"
the trucks cheer.

"Ready? Set? **GO** day!" shouts Jack.

"Ready? Set?
SnOw day!"
cheers Max.

Gabby **skates.**
Kat **Slides.**

Jack shoots.
He SCORES!

Then there is a CRAZY call.

"Do you want an ice cream?
Do you want an ice cream?
Do you want an ice cream?"

Ice Cream

Ice Cream

"Not on a snow day, Izzy," says Jack.

Melvin makes a
snow truck.

Big Rig knocks it down.

Pete dumps.
Pete laughs.

Dan dumps.
Dan laughs last.

SNOWBALL

"Look at that!"
says Jack.

"We cleared ALL
the streets."

Now **THAT** is a Trucktown **snow day.**